TATSINDA

TATSINDA

WRITTEN BY

Elizabeth Enright

ILLUSTRATED BY

Katie Thamer Treherne

An HBJ Contemporary Classic
Harcourt Brace Jovanovich, Publishers
San Diego   New York   London

Library of Congress Cataloging-in-Publication Data
Enright, Elizabeth, 1909–1968.
Tatsinda/by Elizabeth Enright; illustrated by
Katie Thamer Treherne.
p.   cm. — (An HBJ contemporary classic)
Summary: When a giant invades the peaceful kingdom of the
Tatrajanni and takes Tatsinda prisoner, it takes the combined
efforts of the wise woman of the mountain, the Prince, and
Tatsinda herself to rid the kingdom of the intruder.
ISBN 0-15-284280-2
[1. Fairy tales.]   I. Treherne, Katie Thamer, ill.
II. Title.   PZ8.E595Tat   1991
[Fic] — dc20   89-20090

First edition

A B C D E

For three quarters of the Grand Alliance
— E. E.

For Joseph Patrick Ciaran
— K. T. T.

Chapter One

Once upon a time, far, far away at the top of the world, where it is always cold, there was a mountain that no one knew about except the people who lived on it.

The name of the mountain was Tatrajan, and the people who lived on it were called the Tatrajanni. Their many-peaked mountain was so large that it was a country in itself — in fact, it was a kingdom — and because it was warmed by deep interior fires, unlike the other mountains in that frozen region, it was green with forests, pasture valleys, orchards, and gardens. It grew up out of the white wastes like a great green vessel; a vast, elaborate vessel in full sail, and its warmth caused the surrounding ice to dissolve into a wall of mist many miles thick and very high. But within this circle of barrier mist, the sun shone more often than not, and the land of the mountain prospered and flowered.

The king of the Tatrajanni was named King Tagador, and his wife was Queen Tataspan. Their three sons were Prince Tamin, Prince Taskin, and Prince Tackatan. Prince Tackatan was the youngest and most reckless.

It would take a year to describe all the strangeness of the mountain. Things that seemed perfectly natural and ordinary to the Tatrajanni would, from our point of view, be considered very unusual if not almost unbelievable. It would take many pages, for instance, to describe the creatures of the forests and fields. Only a few can be mentioned, among them the appealing timtik, a graceful animal with six delicate legs, hoofs and horns made of a substance resembling mother-of-pearl, a pointed nose like a fox terrier's, and large fan-shaped ears, finely fringed along the edges. It had a musical birdlike call, very pleasing to the ear, and was easily domesticated. Though small, it was extremely strong, and every Tatran child had a timtik to ride to school on. Some of them had two.

There were other creatures: the large, friendly tiptod, which was prized for its milk, though it looked nothing like a cow; more like a flounder with fur. When it traveled across the pastures, the tiptod dipped and ruffled along its edges, resembling a carpet propelled by a strong draft.

There was the small racing tidwell, highly prized by Tatran children as a pet. It looked something like a squirrel but could purr like a kitten and was little enough to fold itself up in a pocket. And then there was the shy, wiry timbertock that skipped along treetops and could fly for short distances. When the moon was bright, it was wakeful, and then one heard it calling in the forest; twanging, rather, since it sounded exactly like the twang of a guitar. The Tatrajanni called these moonlight nights "timbertock nights."

All these animals, and a dozen others not described, had two things in common: fur that was as white as snow and names that began with TI (just as the people all had names that began with TA).

Only among the birds, of which there was a great profusion, would we have recognized some familiar specimens, since these were the only creatures that could come to the mountain from afar and depart at will. No one really wondered where they went; the Tatrajanni's mountain was sufficient for them. The few who had ever felt curiosity enough to go exploring had perished in the wall of mist. It was known that there were poisons there.

As for the trees and flowers and fruits — no, it would take too long to tell about them. It is enough to say that all of them were different from ours: queer, curious, beautiful; *different*.

And the houses of the kingdom were different, too, built as they were of the clouded crystal mined from the mountain: blue, blue-green, gray, and rose. All their roofs were thatched with the scarlet feathers of timaroon birds, a thatch that lasted forever; the weather never wore it out.

Inside of each house, on the warm mountain earth (not too warm; just about as warm as your face is to the touch of your hand) there was a totle. This, which we would call a carpet or a rug, was considered by the Tatrajanni to be as necessary as we would consider a floor, and every house had one, even the poorest.

Each totle was handwoven of fine tiptod fur. (All tiptods were sheared three times a year.) Colored designs were woven into it, many of them very beautiful, and every family took pride in its totles. Most of them had one for each season of the year, and many had more; the royal family, for instance, had nearly a hundred.

At the time of my story the most famous weaver in the kingdom was a young girl named Tatsinda. She had been taught the art of totle-weaving by her foster mother, now dead, and had soon surpassed her in the excellence, originality, and beauty of her design and craftsmanship.

King Tagador bought many of her totles.

"A lucky thing for her, poor girl," he said. "At least she will always have her work, though it certainly is not from pity that I buy it."

Tatsinda was very different from the other inhabitants of the kingdom. She was a beautiful girl, but that was nothing unusual; all Tatran girls were beautiful. The trouble was that her hair was golden and her eyes were brown.

·3·

No one had ever seen anything like it. All the other Tatrajanni — the *true* Tatrajanni — had glittering white hair like snow crystals, and the eyes of every one of them, without exception, were the color of light shining through ice: a cool greenish blue. That was the way people were meant to look, they thought, and they considered Tatsinda handicapped and were sorry for her because of her golden hair and dark eyes.

"Of course no one will ever marry the poor freak," Queen Tataspan said. "She could do something about her hair perhaps; bleach it with tiptod milk or powder it with tel-tel pollen, but what in the mountain could she ever do about her eyes!"

"Well, she is fortunate in having her work," King Tagador said again. "I must say there has never been a totle-weaver to equal her."

Tatsinda was different in appearance because she was the only person in the kingdom who had not been born there. She had come from somewhere beyond the mists: the only creature but the birds who ever had; and then it was a bird who brought her.

One day, sixteen years earlier, an old nobleman named Taxinair had gone hunting in a wild, high region of the mountain. All at once he had seen a flight of eagles winging toward him (tingroks, the Tatrajanni called them), and in the talons of one, gripped by the cloth of her little cloak, was a baby girl about two years old.

Old Taxinair, a splendid huntsman, waited until the eagle was nearly over his head, then, taking careful aim with his todendart, managed to shoot the bird without touching the child. As she plummeted down, he ran forward and was just in time to catch her in his arms.

"And she never cried!" he used to marvel, telling people about this event, as he did for the rest of his life. "She looked at me and smiled and said something in a strange language. Even when she was in the tingrok's claws, she didn't cry!"

Taxinair and his wife, Tabbitina, had never had any children, to their sorrow, and when he took the baby home, Tabbitina welcomed her with delight, fed her and pampered her, and gave her the name she had been saving for

a daughter all these years: Tatsinda, which in the language of the Tatrajanni means "kind and gay."

Tatsinda was a bright, intelligent child who already knew many words, not one of which the old couple could understand; she soon learned their language, however, and talked from morning to night, as happy children are apt to do.

And she *was* happy. The old couple took good care of her and loved her as if she were their own, in spite of her strange appearance.

"I swear I'd just as soon adopt a timbertock, wouldn't you?" one woman said to another at the time. "That dreadful glaring hair, those strange dark eyes; it makes me shudder to look at her. It's terrible to be as sensitive as I am."

"Do you suppose they all look like that beyond the wall of mist?" her friend wondered.

"If so, I'll keep to the mountain, thank you," said the other. "Not that there's the slightest chance of leaving it."

They both laughed happily, thoroughly contented with their life, their kingdom, and their looks.

Tabbitina could guess how people might talk, of course, and being one of the greatest totle-weavers in the land, determined to teach the art to her foster daughter so that not only would she know the pleasure of making beautiful and useful things, but also so that she would have a weapon of excellence to protect her all her life.

And Tatsinda was a willing pupil; more than willing, she was inspired.

"The child has a gift for it," Tabbitina said to Taxinair. "She seems to have been born knowing how to weave."

"Yes, but don't forget she has the finest teacher in all the mountain," Tax-inair reminded his wife. He was very proud of her.

So Tatsinda's life was almost entirely happy. She loved her foster parents and the house they lived in: it was carved of rare crystal the color of peaches; the light that filtered through the walls always seemed warm and comforting, no matter what the weather. She had marvelous toys, a fine timtik to ride on, and two little tidwells for pets. She had her own garden and her own pool,

where fire-colored tinglefins idled or darted. She had a necklace of torms: stones that turned slowly from green to blue, from blue to purple, from purple back to green. The Queen would have been proud of such a necklace.

But sometimes because of her golden hair and brown eyes she was unhappy.

At school, or tokentell as the Tatrajanni called it, on her first day there, the children had stared at her with open curiosity, and some had teased her so that she was close to tears.

It was little Prince Tackatan who came to her rescue.

"Stop that!" he commanded angrily. "Is it her fault that she's funny-looking? Can she help it if her hair is yellow? My father and mother say that even now she weaves better totles than any of the grown-up weavers. . . . And my father and mother are the King and Queen!" he added, sensing that this boast might be of help, as indeed it was. The children stopped their teasing, and it was not long before they accepted her as one of themselves. Though they considered her to be unfortunate in being different, they grew used to her, grew fond of her, and included her in all their games. As for Tatsinda, she loved Prince Tackatan from that day onward.

But as time went by, Tabbitina worried increasingly about her foster daughter's future. She would wake in the night and lie worrying. Sometimes she would even wake up Taxinair so that he could keep her company in worry.

"Now what?" the poor man would groan. "Fretting again about Tatsinda?"

"Yes, I am. We're getting older, Taxinair — "

"Everybody's getting older. Even babies are getting older. Ones that are two days old today will be three days old tomorrow."

"You know what I mean; we're getting older, and someday we'll die. And then what will happen to Tatsinda?"

"She'll go on weaving totles, I suppose," said Taxinair, yawning wearily. "She'll have this fine house to live in, plenty to eat, work to do; so what is there to worry about? Go back to sleep."

"Yes, but she's ten years old already. The years will fly by, and I'm afraid

that she will never marry and she will be lonely. Oh, if only she didn't have that hair and those eyes!"

On and on went Tabbitina; Taxinair had heard it a hundred times. Finally one night, exasperated, he said: "For pity's sake then, Tabbitina, take your troubles to Tanda-nan! Ask *her* advice and let me get some sleep!"

Tabbitina was silent with surprise, and then she said: "That's just exactly what I'll do! Why in the mountain didn't I think of it myself?"

Chapter Two

Tanda-nan, the wise woman of the mountain, lived alone in a high, remote valley. No one knew her age, but since the oldest man in the kingdom could remember that in his childhood Tanda-nan had already been ancient, it seemed likely that she had been alive forever.

She lived very humbly in a cave beside a waterfall. Titchkips (something like chickens, but more intelligent) wandered in and out of the cave, which was furnished with a few sticks of furniture, some pots and pans, and a carved chest. There was no totle on the bare rock floor. Tanda-nan seemed to care nothing for ornaments or objects of beauty. She cared nothing for dress, either. After you had seen her, you could never remember what she had been wearing.

But she was wise in a way that no one else was, and her magic was reliable.

"That is because I use it very seldom," she said. "In this way, it never wears out."

It had long been established as a rule of the kingdom that each of the Tatrajanni would be allowed to ask one question of Tanda-nan; but only one in his whole lifetime.

The consequence was that many a Tatran citizen went through life never

feeling that his situation was grave enough to warrant the asking of the question and so died without. There were others who squandered theirs foolishly. One man, for instance, had demanded to know the whereabouts of a strayed tiptod. "It's back at home," Tanda-nan told him severely. "And if you had stayed there yourself, you would have seen that it rejoined the flock an hour ago." This was true, and the man had used up his question for nothing and could never ask another.

Once a young girl had toiled all the way up the jagged path to inquire if she would ever have a husband.

"Of course you will, you goose," said Tanda-nan. "So go home now and learn to cook."

This sort of foolishness had caused the wise woman to print a message on a rock outside her cave, which said:

> Waste not my time.
> Waste not your own.
> Ask only that
> Which *must* be known.

Reading this, a Tatran would sometimes reconsider, thinking: Well, perhaps after all I had better wait. Perhaps — who knows? — the time will come when my need to use the question will be even greater than now . . .

Then he would turn and start home again, and Tanda-nan, watching him, would say to herself: "There goes a sensible man."

It was a fine, sparkling day when Tabbitina and Tatsinda started out on their journey to the wise woman.

They walked through the town and beyond it across the upland pastures they knew well, and still on, always ascending, through meadows and fields and then wild moorlands; up and up the narrow zigzag path. Chips of crystal rock flashed colored light; the tel-tel flowers were in bloom, sharp triangular white blossoms; above them Tatran butterflies — called tatateens in that country — dipped and sailed and shimmered; blue, every one of them, but many different sorts of blue.

In the far woods, timtiks called sweetly.

Tatsinda skipped and bounded up the path. Then she would stop and wait for Tabbitina to catch up; then skip and bound ahead again.

Tabbitina huffed and grumbled a bit as she climbed.

"I used to *run* up this slope," she complained. "I used to *leap*, just as you are doing now, Tatsinda. 'Time's swiftness makes man's slowness.'"

Tatsinda, waiting on a rock above, said: "I like your slowness. It's the way you are; I like it."

Tabbitina smiled up at her. "Well, you run on now, my wild timtik, my limber timbertock; you run and leap and jump and bound! At your age you're *supposed* to. Don't wait for me."

Tatsinda was glad to obey. She was lively, and the day was bright, the air peculiarly delicious. She went springing up the winding path, and the first thing Tanda-nan saw of her was her bouncing hair, almost blindingly golden in the sunshine.

"What an extraordinary spectacle," said Tanda-nan, who was always talking to herself. Of course she knew who the child was, though she had never seen her before. She knew a great deal about everybody on the mountain.

"Mydeloo, Tatsinda," she called.

Tatsinda stopped short, looking up. The old woman, dressed in a hodge-podge of tatters, seemed the one dark thing on a bright day; but she smiled politely and said: "Mydeloo, Tanda-nan."

("Mydeloo" was the Tatrajanni's way of saying "hello" or "how-do-you-do"; it was a contraction of the more ancient Tatran greeting: "My eye delights in the sight of you.")

"How did you know who I was, Tanda-nan?" inquired Tatsinda, without thinking.

"By the beautiful color of your hair, of course," replied the old woman.

"Beautiful! But no one thinks it's beautiful. They think it's ugly. They think it should be white like theirs, and so do I."

"It's hard for people to understand a beauty they're not used to," Tanda-nan said. "When they get used to it, they will appreciate it."

"And my brown eyes, too?"

"And your brown eyes, too. As for me, I find the sight of them most refreshing. That perpetual, eternal, everlasting, unremitting, undeviating, and unmitigated blue-eyed look becomes monotonous! Downright monotonous!"

While Tatsinda was sorting out the words she understood in this remark, Tabbitina came groaning up the path and joined them.

"Mydeloo, Tanda-nan," she groaned. "Oh, my poor feet; oh, my poor heart; oh, what a terrible climb that is!"

"Come and sit beside the waterfall, and I will bring you a cup of cold telquit nectar," said Tanda-nan.

Tabbitina sank down on a mossy boulder gratefully. Tatsinda picked a tekatu leaf and fanned her mother with it gently.

"That's very refreshing, dear," said Tabbitina. Then she dipped her fingers in the waterfall and dabbed her forehead with the icy drops. "Now I feel like myself again."

Tanda-nan returned with two cups of cold telquit nectar and some tiptod milk with honey in it for Tatsinda. They sat, comfortably sipping and shouting conversation at each other above the noise of the waterfall. Tatsinda was allowed to finish her milk, but the moment she had done so, Tabbitina said: "Now run along, dear; go and play with the titchkips or pick a bunch of teltels or something; Tanda-nan and I have things to talk about."

Tatsinda moved away reluctantly. She did not think the titchkips were very interesting; all they did was warble and prowl and peck at food. There was nothing you could do with them but feed them or chase them.

She wandered across the grass to the largest of the tekatu trees and climbed up into its branches. From high up among the azure leaves, she could look down at the two women, one old and one ancient. She supposed that Tabbitina was about to ask Tanda-nan her lifetime question at last, and being a lively, interested child, she was curious. But she had no intention of eavesdropping; it was only because the two old women, thinking they had lowered their voices, were actually still shouting above the noise of the waterfall. Without meaning to, Tatsinda heard them very well.

"I brought her so that you could see her affliction for yourself," Tabbitina was confiding at the top of her lungs.

"Affliction? You mean the color of her hair and eyes?" Tanda-nan shouted back.

"Why, of course, what else? Poor little creature, she's such a lovely child in every other way. I confess I had hoped in my heart, Tanda-nan — oh, I know how reluctant you are to draw on your sorcery — but I had hoped that just this once you might be persuaded out of pity, out of charity, to practice a little bit of magic to make her hair white and her eyes blue. Couldn't you please, Tanda-nan? So that she will be like other people? So that she will be *normal*?"

Tanda-nan shook her head slowly.

"No, Tabbitina. I never waste my magic on destruction."

"*Destruction?*"

"It would be destruction to alter what is beautiful already. And for all the wrong reasons, too. I'm ashamed of you. The trouble with the people in this mountain is that they are all blinded by custom. They only see what they're used to seeing, so they believe that what they're used to seeing is all that is *worth* seeing. Idiotic. They need to be jolted to a new view; then they would realize that Tatsinda is beautiful in a new way."

Tabbitina sighed and got to her feet. "Well, if you won't, you won't. We must make the best of it . . . But there's one other thing, Tanda-nan. I've never asked you my question. May I ask it now?"

"If you are quite certain that you wish to."

"I am certain," said Tabbitina, but as she and Tanda-nan were moving away from the noise of the waterfall, they really did lower their voices, and Tatsinda never heard the question or the answer.

On the way back, winding down the crooked path, Tatsinda walked thoughtfully beside Tabbitina instead of leaping and jumping.

"Why has Tanda-nan no totle?" she asked finally.

"Well, I don't know," Tabbitina replied. "Totles belong in houses, and I doubt if you can call a cave a house."

"I think I'll weave one for her," Tatsinda said.

Tabbitina thought it was nice for Tatsinda to be generous, though she was by no means sure that Tanda-nan would be pleased by the gift of a totle. The bony discomforts of her home seemed to suit her.

Tabbitina was wrong, however.

A few weeks later when Tatsinda had completed the totle, she did it up in a bundle, strapped it on her back like a knapsack, and trudged the long way up the path. The sun was hot; the bundle heavy. By the time she had reached the high valley, she was panting and dripping.

Old Tanda-nan, surrounded by her flock of titchkips, was gathering tef-fets — a sort of mushroom — for her dinner.

"Mydeloo, Tanda-nan," called Tatsinda.

The old woman saw her and straightened up. "Mydeloo, child," she answered. "But you know the question can't be asked by people less than twelve years old."

"But I haven't come to ask it," replied Tatsinda. "I have woven you a totle for a present because I thought you needed one."

She threw down the bundle with a sigh of relief, then opened it and spread it on the grass; snowy white, with a pattern of blue timbertocks around the edge, alive and leaping.

"Why, Tatsinda . . . why, it's beautiful . . ." said Tanda-nan, for once almost at a loss for words. "It's so beautiful!"

She inched her old self down and put out her brindled hand to stroke the silky surface of the totle.

"Rock is a cold floor," she said. "All my life I've wanted one of these."

"I'll help you move your furniture and put it down," Tatsinda offered, feeling proud of her handiwork.

And when the totle was spread out on the floor of the cave, warm and bright, the wise woman's home seemed a different place; in every way more pleasant.

The titchkips, one by one, began prowling in to see what was going on.

"Shoo! Scat! Out!" cried Tanda-nan, springing at them. "Stay off my totle from now on! Stay outdoors!"

When it was time for Tatsinda to leave, the old woman accompanied her to where the path began.

"Child," said Tanda-nan, "when the day comes for you to ask your question, I want you to remember that I am going to make you a present of a little magic; just enough to make one wish come true."

"But Tanda-nan," cried Tatsinda. "That isn't why I gave you the totle: so that you would give a present back to me!"

"I know, I know," the wise woman hastened to say. "Just the same, remember what I have told you. You may be glad of it one day."

Tatsinda thanked her warmly and promised to remember. Then she went running and singing down the path. Without the bundle on her back she felt lighter than a leaf.

Chapter Three

Now, on the other side of the wall of mist and well beyond it, unknown to the Tatrajanni, there lived a tribe of creatures called the Gadblangs. They were huge, extremely ugly beings, more like trolls than anything else, though actually they had no troll blood. They hated daylight, living in dark tunnels and grottoes under the ice and rocks, never coming out until night, and not then if the moon was full.

They were a miserly, greedy lot. All their waking lives were spent in mining for a precious mineral called greb. Greb ore was collected, then heated and beaten into thin wafer-shaped disks or plates. It was the ambition of every Gadblang to have more greb than anybody else, and to this end not only did they work themselves to the bone, but also thievery, cheating, and battle were common in their nation.

The continual pounding and ringing of their picks and axes, hammers and anvils, had influenced their language; all their names had a bang and racket to them. Their leader, for instance, was called Johrgong, and his henchmen were Blamrigg, Clangmar, and Gagg. They were all ugly, but Johrgong was the ugliest, which was one reason why he was the leader. Another reason was that he had managed to grab more greb plates than anybody else and kept them

well hidden, too. He was a giant, with a great lunging head, a deep voice, and a cruel heart. Like the other Gadblangs, he wore leather clothes and shoes of stone. When a group of Gadblangs ran along their mighty stone passages in their mighty stone shoes, the din was beyond imagining; it could be heard for miles about, startling the snow animals and raising the birds. Sometimes even the Tatrajanni could hear it and supposed it to be a distant storm.

While the Gadblangs loathed the daylight and all light of the outer world, they did not mind the sight of their own murky fires or the bright sparks flying from red-hot anvils. And the reflected glow on the polished surface of a greb plate was the one beauty they recognized.

Their only fear was that the day might come when all greb had been mined from the earth, and what would they do then?

It happened at this time that on the mountain of Tatrajan there was a visiting owl named Skoodoon. He was a great snowy owl with a round head, feathery leggings, yellow eyes, and a furious beak. He was not visiting because he wished to but because a blizzard had blown him a hundred miles off his course. When he finally emerged from it, he was so blinded by the sudden Tatran sunlight that he flew into a rock and broke his wing and was forced to stay where he was until it mended.

He was an unreasonable, cranky bird, never accepting the blame for anything, and so he conceived a mighty grudge against the mountain and all that was on it. The rock, he felt, had deliberately apprehended him in order to break his wing. The blizzard, sent by the mountain, had deliberately sought him out to do him damage.

Also there was none of the sort of thing he liked to eat there: no rabbits, no mice, no small rodents of any kind. He could not abide the taste of tidwells and was confined to a diet of berries and seeds, much to his displeasure.

Another thing was that nobody understood his language. The Gadblangs did. In fact, at the time of his accident he had been on his way to pay them a visit, feeling a sudden wish to feast on greb rats, a delicacy in which the Gadblangs' caves abounded. It was true that he always had to bargain for this privilege; the Gadblangs did not like to let go of anything anyone else wanted, even a rat. But though disagreeable, Skoodoon was a shrewd, intelligent bird and usually managed to get his way.

Now, stuck here in this outlandish place and enduring a diet of sparrow food, he kept his eyes open, at least at night, and noticed certain things that might be useful to him later.

And indeed this proved to be so.

One dark night when his wing was entirely healed, Skoodoon set forth from Tatrajan on his journey to the Gadblangs. He flew silently and swiftly, without tiring (he had exercised his wing daily), feeling both the exultation of flight and a rising appetite for the taste of greb rat.

Fuming and curling far below, the wall of mist seemed almost endless. Dark though it was, Skoodoon had owl's eyes and could see it.

But at last he had left it behind and, on reaching the mountains and ravines of Gadblang territory, he slackened his flight and circled about.

This was the sort of night in which the Gadblangs sometimes walked abroad; and there, sure enough, Skoodoon saw one now lumbering over the snow, and from the immense size of the creature he knew it to be Johrgong.

Narrowing the circle of his flight, Skoodoon dropped, landing soft as an eiderdown muff right in the giant's path.

"Gettonemy, Johrgong," the owl greeted him.

"Gettonemy, bird," replied Johrgong grudgingly.

("Gettonemy" was the Gadblangs' way of saying "hello"; it was a contraction of the more ancient Gadblang greeting: "Get out of here if you're my enemy.")

"Well, what do you want now?" Johrgong inquired in his cordial way.

"I want to hunt greb rats whenever I wish to. No restrictions," replied Skoodoon in a businesslike tone.

"*What?*" roared Johrgong, startled at this audacity. "Who says we want to give our greb rats away? Who says we don't want them for ourselves?"

"And who said anything about giving them away?" Skoodoon countered. "What I propose is an exchange of accommodations."

Fortunately, Johrgong understood the word "exchange" if not the word

"accommodations" and came at once to the point.

"What do you offer?" he said.

Skoodoon fixed him with his yellow eye. He ruffed his feathers out, then flattened them again.

"Greb," he said. "More greb, Johrgong, than you could ever hope to carry. Or than all the other Gadblangs could carry."

"Leave the other Gadblangs out of this," commanded Johrgong. "Where is the greb you speak of? Lead me to it."

"Not so fast," said Skoodoon. "First we must have a legal understanding concerning the disposition of greb rats."

"After you have led me to the greb," promised Johrgong.

"On the contrary," stated Skoodoon. "Before. And even before *that*, I must ease my hunger with a few at once. For three weeks, now, I have lived on thorns and husks and garden trash, and *I want meat!*"

He was so determined that Johrgong saw there was nothing for it but to let him have his way. And after that, matters were further delayed, because having gorged himself atrociously on greb rat, Skoodoon was so stupefied that he slept for fourteen hours.

"But now," roared Johrgong finally, shaking him by the wing. "Now keep your part of the bargain! Do you hear? The contract has been drawn up; you may hunt greb rat whenever you wish. But *you* keep *your* part of the bargain now!"

So Skoodoon, between yawns, described how in the kingdom of Tatrajan the greb lay shining in the roads and fields and paths: pebbles and stones of purest greb that no one paid attention to, unless sometimes they paved a street with it.

"They regard it as gravel," Skoodoon said. "Worthless stuff, really. There's more than enough for all of you."

"All of us, nothing! Enough for *me*," Johrgong declared. "I've sent Blam-rigg, Clangmar, and Gagg on an errand to the Blongrack Bog; they won't be back for a week. And they are never to know, do you understand? No one is to know of the new greb source but you and me; and if you ever let the secret out,

I will wring your miserable neck!"

Skoodoon glanced at Johrgong's hands, huge and hard as iron shovels, but he spoke most calmly.

"Alter your tone, please, Johrgong," he said. "Remember, if you can, that we are partners in an enterprise. Remember also that my taste for greb rat is a powerful factor in my maintaining silence."

"Well, all right," said Johrgong sulkily. "How far away is this mountain?"

"Roughly fifty owl-leagues, I should say. I don't know what that is in Gadblang-leagues," replied Skoodoon. "But far less than a night of traveling should do it. I realize, of course, that you must travel by night. Luckily you are a giant, and the poison vapors in the wall of mist won't trouble you. They lie low. The birds found that out long ago; the ones who flew too low were killed. And that is why the Tatrajanni — tiny, compared to you — stay isolated in their kingdom."

As soon as it was dark that evening, the two set out for Tatrajan, the giant tramping with a gonglike tread in his stone shoes; the white owl circling and sailing quietly about his head.

After an hour or so they came to the beginning of the wall of mist; very high it looked and very strange. Johrgong hesitated. This was the farthest he had ever traveled aboveground.

"Bird, you would not betray me, would you?" he demanded suddenly.

"That is not worthy of you. Are you afraid?" inquired Skoodon, lighting on Johrgong's yoke. (The giant was wearing a yoke on his shoulders, from each end of which hung a gigantic basket.)

Johrgong sighed with a sound like that of a train coming into a station. Then he plunged into the mist. The owl flew beside him, now and then rising high up into the clear air to make certain of his bearings, then descending to direct and encourage his companion.

It was a curious experience to walk through the wall of mist. It was cold, cold, cold, and almost suffocatingly dense in there. And still! There never was such stillness; a terrible stillness that seemed almost to be alive, almost to be listening . . .

It got on Johrgong's nerves so badly that he started to sing the Greb Song just for the sake of the noise:

> Clang the hammer, strike the floor,
> Slam the anvil, free the or...
> Fireshine-red and ours alone!
> This I swear as e'er I swore:
> By sundered head and sundered stone,
> By aching arms and breaking backs,
> By broken pick and broken bone,
> By broken vow and broken ax,
> By biting, fighting, hate, and toil,
> Almighty Greb shall be our own!
> Fireshine-red and ours alone;
> Alone our prize, alone our spoil!
> Greb! Greb! Greb! Greb! Greb!

But Johrgong's voice, though somewhat muffled by the fog, got on Skoodoon's nerves so badly that he said: "If you do that again, I'll do this," and he released his war scream, a most terrible and paralyzing sound.

After that for a long time, except for the mighty pounding of Johrgong's stony shoes, they were silent.

But at last the giant stopped dead in his tracks, trembling.

"Skoodoon! I see light ahead! Get me into darkness quickly! If the sun rises in my sight, I'm ruined!"

"That is not the sun," the owl said reassuringly. "Those are the lights of Tatrajan. We are nearly there; no doubt the people have already heard your footsteps. Step loudly now, Johrgong, as loudly as you can, and sing the Greb Song at full voice. It will not hurt to frighten them a little."

Chapter Four

Meanwhile, on Tatrajan, eight years had passed since Tatsinda's visit to the wise woman. They had been very happy years until the sixth; and then one night Tabbitina and Taxinair lay down hand in hand to go to sleep and never woke up again.

Tatsinda grieved bitterly for her foster parents, though they had been very old, with a fine, long life behind them and almost no troubles to remember.

And they had provided well for their daughter, leaving her the house of peach crystal, the lovely gardens, the animals, and all else that they had valued. So Tatsinda finally took up her life again, continuing her studies at the tokentell, continuing her friendships, continuing her weaving, and continuing to love Prince Tackatan in silence. He had grown up to be the handsomest of young men and, in addition, was strong, brave, generous, and clever. It was another grief to Tatsinda to learn, as she did at this time, that he had been betrothed since the age of one week to a beautiful girl named Tamberine.

Tamberine was a perfect example of Tatran beauty; her eyes the iciest blue-green, her snow-crystal hair the snowiest and curliest. Tatsinda could not help envying this girl and, watching her, mourned anew her own strange coloring. But most of all she envied Tamberine for her betrothal to Prince

Tackatan, even though this betrothal had been arranged for the young couple before they could walk or talk and had nothing to do with their own choosing.

The knowledge of the latter fact gave Tatsinda a little hope, though she realized the hope was based more on wish than possibility. Who in the mountain would ever want to marry a girl with brown eyes and golden hair?

Still, she could not help thinking of the prince. She thought of him all day long, and at night she dreamed of him. She watched with delight when he excelled at the stone-balancing game, tenbolt, and listened with delight when he played the tetrina, an instrument something like a flute. And sometimes, too, she thought she saw him watching her.

At last she decided she must go to Tanda-nan and ask her lifetime question.

On the chosen day — a day that looked lucky, it was so fine — Tatsinda left her house, walked through the village and the upland fields, and soon was climbing the mountain path. It zigzagged steeply between thorny tegleg bushes all hung now with lantern-shaped green flowers. These had a wonderful wild scent unlike anything else in the world. The Tatrajanni were in the habit of drying them and putting them in their pillows; the fragrance was supposed to cause fortunate dreams and was good for the health.

Above the small snarled bushes a thousand butterflies dipped and flitted in a speckled blue veil.

When Tatsinda turned and looked down, she saw a strange wild scene. Great valleys and pastures descended in broad, gigantic terraces. Far beyond and below were the timaroon-crimson rooftops of the town, and still farther beyond was the wall of mist, always stirring and breathing like a weightless ocean; like an ocean of smoke. But overhead the air was pure, blue, cloudless, marked only by birds traveling their paths.

All down the mountainside small streams shattered and mended themselves among the crystal rocks, and on their banks the water-loving tondil flower nodded its lily head.

It was such a lovely day that Tatsinda would have been happy if it had not been for the burden of her question. Suppose the answer should be sad?

Sometimes it had to be. When I come down this path, will I be walking slowly and sorrowfully, she wondered; or will I be leaping and dancing as I did the last time I was here?

She could smell the smoke of Tanda-nan's cook fire long before she was in sight of it. But at last, with her heart beating hard, and not only because of the climb, she reached the valley where the wise woman lived.

Tanda-nan sat in the sun, spinning.

"Mydeloo, Tatsinda," she called. "Welcome indeed! Why, what a beautiful young person you've become!"

"Thank you, thank you," said Tatsinda, hardly noticing. "Oh, Tanda-nan, I've come at last to ask my question!" She was surprised to find that she was trembling as she knelt down by the old woman.

"Be careful now," Tanda-nan warned her. "Don't waste it! Are you perfectly, absolutely, positively, incontrovertibly, and indubitably certain that you wish to ask this question now?"

"Perfectly certain," replied Tatsinda, still trembling.

"Very well then. Let me hear it," said the old woman, putting her work aside.

So Tatsinda asked from her heart if she might ever hope to be the bride of Tackatan.

"Aha," said Tanda-nan. "I thought as much. I *thought* as much. Well, I can tell you this. It is possible. It is *just* possible. Because, if you remember, Tatsinda, I promised you a present of magic; enough to make one wish come true. But," she added, forestalling Tatsinda's expression of joy. "*But* you will have to work the spell yourself. All I can do is to give you the directions."

"Anything!" cried Tatsinda. "I will do anything you say!"

"Well, it's really quite simple," Tanda-nan continued. "As you know, the prince's eighteenth birthday will fall on the next first day of the dark of the moon, and you and everybody else will go to the celebration at the palace. I've been asked myself, but I have a previous engagement. Now this is what you must do, and you haven't much time, either. You must weave a totle for the prince's birthday present. Into the design, very subtly, so that nobody will notice, you are to weave three of the golden hairs of your head. Then you will present this totle to the prince. And after that we shall see!"

"But will it really work? Really, really, truly?" begged Tatsinda.

"I never dilute my magic," Tanda-nan said stiffly. She did not care for doubt. But in the next moment she softened. "I think I can promise that you will have your wish," she said.

"Oh, Tanda-nan, how happy you have made me!" cried Tatsinda, seizing the old woman's hand and kissing it warmly.

Then she was required to draw three long golden hairs from her head. These Tanda-nan took in her hand, turned her back to Tatsinda, and said a word that sounded like:

"T Z X W Q P Z T X N Q P N Z T X."

After that she wrapped the hairs in a tekatu leaf and gave them to Tatsinda, saying: "Do not lose them!"

As Tatsinda made her way down the mountain path, she noticed that she was walking slowly; and it was not from sorrow but because she felt too happy to run.

It was true that there was not much time before the prince's birthday; but Tatsinda worked willingly day and night, weaving and weaving and singing as she wove.

And when it was finished, at the very last minute, the totle was a thing of great beauty: warm, rich, dazzling in design. Three fire-colored tinglefins swam a diagonal course across the fabric. Each wore a royal circlet on its head, and into the gold of each circlet a single strand of Tatsinda's golden hair was woven so skillfully that nobody would ever know it but herself.

As the hour of the celebration approached, she put on her most beautiful dress and her necklace of torms, picked up the package containing the totle, and hurried to the palace. It was bravely lighted and gleaming like a sapphire, being carved of blue translucent crystal; and already it was ringing with music.

In Tatrajan on royal birthdays, and, in fact, on *all* birthdays from the

eighteenth onward, it was the custom for the guest of honor to dance and feast with the other guests the whole night through and to open his presents only in the very first light of the sun. Tatsinda added her present to the great pyramid of others and turned to the dancing.

She danced and danced; and more than once Prince Tackatan chose her as partner.

But at the height of the merriment one keen-eared Tatran paused, went to the door, and leaned out.

"Hush!" he commanded, turning back into the room and raising his hand. "Listen, all of you! Listen!"

The musicians ceased their playing. The guests fell silent. The king and queen on their thrones turned pale; then everyone turned pale.

For what was the terrible strange sound they heard? A sound as loud as thunder; but thunder that was spaced, measured, rhythmic, like unimaginable footsteps: rock-shuddering, gonglike footsteps pounding closer . . . and closer . . . and closer . . .

"Is it coming from the mountain?" cried the people. "Is it coming from the sky?"

"No," said Tackatan, the prince. "It is coming from within the wall of mist!"

Now, suddenly, added to the pounding steps, was the sound of a great rough voice raised up in song: an unbelievable and ghastly clamor! The Tatrajanni poured through the palace doors and stood in the night's darkness, lanterns raised high, staring powerless at the barrier mist, waiting for that which must emerge.

And soon, vaguely at first in the swirling fogs, then more clearly and boldly, they beheld the awesome spectacle of Johrgong the giant, with his yoke and baskets, and the white owl hovering about his head.

Once again a bird had brought a stranger to the mountain from the outer world.

Chapter Five

Among the Tatrajanni war was unknown. They sometimes quarreled among themselves, sometimes argued, but it was as the members of a happy family sometimes quarrel and argue. It was always over soon, and nobody got hurt.

Therefore, though awed by the immense size of the giant and somewhat stunned by his ugliness, they approached him in an attitude of friendship.

"Mydeloo!" cried Tackatan, advancing with his arms raised in greeting. Not quite sure of how to address this stranger, he added: "Mydeloo, O you who come from within the wall of mist, or from beyond it, or wherever you do come from."

"Mydeloo!" echoed all the Tatrajanni, the king and queen included. "Welcome!" they called, looking up at Johrgong's face and smiling.

Johrgong's response was to kick in the wall of a house. Then he bent down, brushed six timtiks aside with his hand, or rather knocked them sprawling, and scooped up a handful of stones.

"Greb!" he roared. "Greb, Skoodoon! Greb unlimited! You have spoken well and truly!"

The Tatrajanni, shocked and unable to believe their eyes, watched as the giant clawed up the rocks and pebbles of their roads, yanked at their paving stones, grabbed up the boulders in their gardens.

"Greb!" he roared again, baring all of his ninety-seven teeth in a blood-curdling smile of cheer. "I am happy, Skoodoon! I am overwhelmed with joy, O noble Skoo! Now I shall be the richest Gadblang in all Blangdom! I shall have more greb than anyone in the world!"

And at this, nearly crazy with delight, Johrgong executed a few dance steps, causing the earth to shudder and several chimneys to topple. Alarmed, the distant tiptod flocks howled melodiously in their pastures.

Gloating and beaming, Johrgong sifted the precious greb into one of his huge baskets. Then suddenly, and for the first time, he took full notice of the Tatrajanni who, though just as large as regular people, seemed infinitesimal to the giant.

"What curious small oddities!" he said contemptuously. "Smaller than greb rats, aren't they? Almost as small as greb *mice!* They all look exactly alike too: white-haired, yet not old; and all so disgustingly *pretty.* What dreadful and repulsive little creatures! Very stupid, too, obviously, since they do not realize the worth of greb. See how they allow it to lie about, pave their streets with it, let animals walk over it! How stupid! I abominate such stupidity."

"And yet you gain by it," Skoodoon reminded him. "Here it lies for the taking, all yours."

"True enough, true enough," gloated Johrgong, smiling his horrible smile again. "I shall enjoy my visit here. These creatures, though . . . What do you call them? The Tatrajanni? . . . Will they be troublesome, do you suppose?"

"Your precious greb is trash to them," Skoodoon replied. "And observe the size of them, besides. How could they trouble *you?*"

"They are very small," Johrgong agreed. "So small and so similar . . . But wait! Look! Here's one of a different sort entirely!" And with surprising swift-ness the giant leaned over, plucked Tatsinda from the ground, and lifted her dizzyingly to the level of his gaze. "See, Skoodoon; her eyes are the right color: dark as night, and her hair — how it shines — is almost as bright as polished greb! This one I shall take home for my little niece to play with."

It was true that Johrgong had a niece at home, a seven-year-old giantess

named Jangborg. Already she was the size of a small house and ugly enough to startle a cow into convulsions, but since among the Gadblangs ugliness was considered a mark of the highest distinction, let no one feel sorry for her.

"How dear little Jangborg will enjoy pulling out this dolly's hair," Johrgong said lovingly. "How she will enjoy toasting her little feet on a red-hot anvil!"

Fortunately for Tatsinda, she could not understand a word of Johrgong's language, and neither could any of the other Tatrajanni; but they understood from his actions that this creature had not come as a friend but as an enemy: a word which, in their tongue, had never been invented until now. And they were horrified to see Tatsinda in his clutch. Those who remembered the old tale of Tatsinda's arrival in Tatrajan remembered that she had not cried though carried in a tingrok's claws; nor was she crying now.

"Try not to be afraid," called Prince Tackatan. "We will come to your rescue!" And somehow Tatsinda managed to smile at him.

Then the prince turned to the crowd and commanded: "Fellow Tatrans, prepare your todendarts. This creature means us harm!"

A gasp ran through the crowd. As I have said, war was unknown to them. Their todendarts were used for adornment and the purpose of hunting; never had a Tatran turned this weapon on a fellow being. Never had such a thing been dreamed of; and this monster towering above them, though he tore up their paving blocks, kicked in the walls of their houses, and, but for their agility, would have crushed them themselves with his stone boots, was still, like themselves, a two-legged creature: a mortal being. They hesitated.

King Tagador tried another tactic. He stepped forward from the throng, every inch the king.

"Unknown person from beyond the mist, control yourself!" he ordered. "Put the maiden down again and mend your manners or begone!"

Though Johrgong did not understand these words, he sensed their meaning and, looking down at Tagador, he laughed scornfully and with the edge of his stone shoe pushed the king sideways until he was pressed against the palace wall.

That was too much.

"Men, take aim!" commanded Tackatan; and all the Tatran men raised their weapons and took careful aim.

"Now, fire!" snapped Tackatan.

Todendart bolts, hundreds of them, spun upward like a fury of wasps. But when they struck the giant's leather clothes, they bounced away and fell harmless to the ground, and when they stung his hands and face, it was only with the little sting of salt spray. Johrgong looked surprised, and then he laughed.

"Aha, and so it's war they want!" he shouted happily. He loved a battle dearly.

But Skoodoon flew down and lighted on his shoulder.

"Why divert yourself from the main issue, Johrgong?" he said. "A fracas will only cause delay and be a nuisance. Let us not lose sight of our objective. I know a place high on the mountain where there is a veritable quarry of greb. First-quality greb, Johrgong, shining like the morning sun!"

"Do not use that word to me!" said the giant, scowling; but in a moment he smiled again. "Is it a large quarry, Skoodoon?"

"A splendid size," the owl assured him. "Now put the maiden down, will you, and let us be on our way."

But here Johrgong was stubborn. "No," he said. "I want my niece to have this lively dolly, and she shall have her. You are not to let her out of your sight while I am working, Skoodoon; you are to find food for her and weave a tether to keep her from running away."

"I did not bargain for that," the owl said crossly. "But all right, if you insist, and now finally let us go!"

The poor Tatrajanni, helpless for the moment, scattered before the giant's tramping shoes; but Tackatan ran after them.

"Tatsinda!" he called, "I will save you yet! I will find a way to save you."

"I have faith in you, my prince," Tatsinda called in reply.

And then Johrgong's mighty stride outdistanced the running of Tackatan.

The owl, the giant, and Tatsinda, captive in the giant's clasp, all vanished in the black of night.

Chapter Six

Four days and four nights passed; four days of worry and distress in the kingdom of Tatrajan; four nights of sleeplessness or fearful dreams. In the palace Prince Tackatan's pyramid of presents stood untouched. He had neither heart nor time to open them. Each day from dawn to dark he and his brothers, with all the other able-bodied Tatran men, searched for the giant. They sought him in the wildest regions of the mountain; on barren heaths, in forested ravines, among the crystal pillars of the Tondil Glades; but never a trace of him did they see.

The wise woman, of course, had been consulted at once. Prince Tackatan had been chosen to go to her and ask her aid; and when at last he had reached the high valley, which was her abode, he had found her standing at the head of the path as though she had been waiting for him.

"Mydeloo, my prince," she said. "I know that there is trouble in the kingdom. Sit down and rest beside the waterfall and tell me the whole story."

So Tackatan described the dreadful visitation and said in conclusion: "My brothers and I have vowed that we will never cease our search until Tatsinda has been rescued and the giant banished from the mountain or rendered harmless. But we need your help, O Tanda-nan. The giant is too strong for us. Is it possible that there is a magic you could bring to our aid? The need is desperate."

Tanda-nan frowned thoughtfully.

"Why, yes, I think perhaps there is," she said in a moment. "Of course it has never been applied to a giant, or to any other creature from beyond the mist, for that matter; but it worked very well with the timbledads." (The timbledads, ferocious beasts something like hoofed polar bears, had been extinct on Tatrajan for centuries.) "My greatest-great-grandmother, the one who baked and brewed these magics in the first place, thought very highly of this one. She considered it her major work, in fact. Excuse me for a moment."

Tanda-nan disappeared in her cave and was soon heard rummaging and crackling among the packets of magic she kept in the old carved chest. When she returned, she was rather dusty and carrying an antique box.

"The words printed on this box," said Tanda-nan, "were put there by my greatest-great-grandmother (in archaic Tatraic, of course), and they say: 'To be used only on occasions of total desperation.'"

"Well, such an occasion has arisen," Tackatan said. "We *are* desperate."

"I know, I know. Now look, my prince," commanded Tanda-nan. "Look in quickly; the magic must not evaporate."

She opened the box, and Tackatan saw a heap of turquoise-colored powder before she snapped it shut again.

"Now this is what you must do," continued Tanda-nan. "You, and you alone, must somehow make a circle of this powder on the ground around the giant. I don't know how you are ever going to do it. First of all, you have to find him, naturally, and it would help if you could find him asleep, but failing that —"

"Failing that, I will manage somehow," Tackatan said grimly. "I will because I must. And what effect will the magic have on the giant?"

"It will turn him into music," said Tanda-nan.

"*Music!*" cried Tackatan. "How can anyone so horrible become anything so pleasant as a tune?"

"I did not say it would be pleasant," replied the wise woman. "It will be a

base and trumpery air, more likely; a dissonant and vulgar farrago. Earsplitting, as well. But it hardly matters. The music will play itself right away from the mountain and into the endless snow, and nobody will ever hear it but the northern lights!"

"An admirable solution; ingenious and humane," said Tackatan, standing up and reaching for the box.

"One moment, please. I must tell you, my prince, that this is all the powder there is. Be very sure before you use it!"

Tackatan promised that he would be, thanked her, and departed to rejoin the searchers.

It was on the afternoon of the fifth day, and quite by chance, that the prince discovered the giant's hiding place.

He had become separated from his companions and now found himself in a part of the mountain with which he was fairly unfamiliar. It was a wooded region, shadowy and still. There was no breeze that day: every leaf on every tree hung motionless, and all the timbertocks were sleeping.

Tackatan, deep in thought, made his way down the mountainside. He was very light of foot and quiet; all Tatran people were quiet-footed, and their shoes were woven of thick tempkin floss and lined with the down of timaroon birds. So, through the silent wood the prince moved silently.

But after a time he began to be aware of a sound; a strangely rhythmic sound, something between a snarl, a rumble, and a purr. Very curious. It reminded him of something, but he couldn't think what.

He followed the sound, which grew louder and louder as he progressed until it was appalling. It led him at last to a clearing and, emerging from the wood, he saw that he was on the edge of a large gravel pit or quarry. Someone had been busy there, quarrying the brightly shining but tawdry stones of triknix. (That which the Gadblangs prized and called "greb," the Tatrajanni considered worthless and called "triknix.") Tackatan noticed this with but fleeting attention, however, because what astonished him was the fact that the noise seemed to be coming from the center of the quarry and *from under the*

earth! Or at least from under the gigantic blue quartz boulder that was lying there. The noise was now prodigious. Even brave Tackatan felt a little fear as he approached the rock.

Something white lay on the ground at his feet, and in the instant that he recognized it as a white owl's feather, he knew that he had stumbled on the giant's refuge.

So, it is the sound of snoring I hear! thought Tackatan; so loud that I didn't recognize it for what it was. I've found the giant's sleeping place, just as Tanda-nan hoped. It is almost too good to be true — unless, he suddenly thought with horror, unless Tatsinda should also be under that rock!

He looked anxiously about, and presently, to his great relief, he spied Tatsinda lying fast asleep beneath a tree. She was tethered to the tree, he saw, by a long cord, and even in sleep her face looked pale and sad. On a branch above her the great white guardian owl was also fast asleep, his head well muffled by his wing. She is still safe, the prince thought gratefully, and soon now she will know it. It would not do to wake her yet; first let the giant be dealt with and, after that, the owl.

Opening the box of magic, Tackatan began to circle the boulder on tiptoe, allowing plenty of space and scattering the turquoise powder on the ground. The noise of Johrgong's sleep was thunderous; yet when the prince's foot dislodged a rattling pebble, the rumbling ended with a mighty snort. Under the boulder there was a sudden suspicious, listening silence. Tackatan froze in his tracks, hardly breathing. The white owl muttered in his wing; Tatsinda flung her arm across her eyes; but neither woke. After a while — and it seemed a very long while — the giant was heard to yawn and murmur something in his native tongue. The boulder rocked a little as, presumably, he rolled over, and soon the mighty noise began again.

With infinite care and stealth the prince completed the magic circle; then he hid himself in a clump of tetrapin bushes close to Tatsinda and waited, prepared to wait all night if necessary. He had never seen anyone turn into music.

During the time she had been stolen by the giant, Tatsinda had been forced to adopt his habits: to sleep in the daytime, as he and Skoodoon did, and to stay awake at night while they were working. Never was she loosed from her tether, though it was long enough to admit a certain amount of wandering. And never for more than a few minutes at a time was she out of the sight of Skoodoon's eye. Being suspicious and a tattletale by nature, the owl made an excellent guard, at least from Johrgong's point of view. Tatsinda's few attempts at escape had been instantly reported to the giant by the conniving bird, and she was beginning to fear that Tackatan might never find her; that the prospect of liberty might be closed to her forever.

And how she longed for her liberty! At night while Johrgong was busy and the owl made his short forays in search of food, Tatsinda would pace back and forth as far as the tether would allow her, or she would sit quietly on the dewy grass. She breathed the fresh, sweet air of the night world: the scent of the mountain fields and woods, and sometimes between the noises of Johrgong's choppings and scrapings she could hear a night bird or the distant twanging of a timbertock.

Village lights were scattered far below — ah, how she longed to be among them! — and overhead more often than not the aurora borealis washed the sky with color: vast shuddering veils and canopies of light, pierced through and through with small fierce stars.

Tatsinda, who had wept seldom in her life, could not help weeping sometimes on these nights.

But beyond the fact of being captive against her will, she was not treated badly. Skoodoon performed his duties reliably, bringing her food: teffets and tempkins and the delicious fruit of the telquit tree, which was ripe at that season. This fruit the owl enjoyed himself; it was the only vegetarian food he did enjoy, and he brought it back in great quantity. Every evening, too, he was scrupulous about bringing Tatsinda a tempkin rind filled with clear spring water. Between these errands of duty he hunted for himself, finding little beyond the telquit fruit to vary the monotonous Tatran diet. Toward sunrise of the fourth day he was becoming restive.

"Johrgong," he said. "You have been imposing on my patience. I had not bargained for more than a night in this forsaken place, two at the most. And here it is already the fourth! I've fed your beastly doll for you and kept her safe for four mortal nights, and I would remind you now that I am not a nursemaid, Johrgong — I'm an *owl*! I want to fly where I want to fly! I want to go back to the greb caves and eat rat! *I want meat!*"

"Only a little longer," begged Johrgong in a whining voice. "Only the night that is coming, Skoo, and the one after that. Just two tiny nights more."

"But why?" cried Skoodoon, ruffing his feathers in exasperation. "Already you've collected twenty times more greb than your baskets can carry! Is there no end to your cupidity?"

"Listen, Skoodoon," Johrgong said. "I can't leave all this gorgeous greb behind, can I? So what I plan is to build a sledge and load it. Then I will *drag* it down the mountain, *drag* it across the horrid little villages, squashing them, *drag* it through the mist and across the ice to home. When Blamrigg, Clangmar, and Gagg see what *I've* got, they will break their heads against the wall in a fury of envy. Oh, what a lovely and delightful thought!" Again Johrgong did his little dance of joy. The earth shook, and three timbertocks fell out of a tree.

"And anyway," he added, "I *can't* stay any longer than two more nights. The new moon refuses to stay new; each night the cursed thing grows brighter, and I cannot wait till it is dark again. Already Blamrigg and the others will be hunting for my greb store."

"Well, I suppose I can support the tedium another night or two," Skoodoon said unwillingly. "But you'd better go to earth, now, Johrgong. The sky grows lighter, and soon the sun will rise."

Cursing the sun, Johrgong rolled into the hollow he had dug for himself and then reached out and pulled the boulder into place, like a roof or lid, so that he was safe from daylight.

Skoodoon flew to his perch in the tree, shook out his wing, fluffed it up invitingly, and tucked his head into it.

Tatsinda stayed awake to watch the sun come up. And with its rising, beautiful and bright, she felt hope rising in her heart.

This was the day on which, much later, Tackatan discovered Johrgong's sleeping place.

Hidden by tetrapin leaves, the prince did not have to wait long before the day grew dimmer. At last he saw the evening star.

The white owl was the first to wake. He shook himself out, ruffed his feathers, did a little preening, trimmed a claw, and snapped his beak vigorously a few times to sharpen it. Then he swooped from the branch like a huge white shadow and drifted off to find some breakfast.

"Tatsinda!" said the prince in a low voice. "Tatsinda, wake up!"

Tatsinda started up and looked about her, believing she had dreamed the prince's voice.

"It is I, Tackatan," he said. "I am here in the tetrapin bushes. I have set a magic for the giant, Tatsinda. As soon as he pushes away the boulder and stands up, the magic will work, and after that you will be free, my dear Tatsinda, and I will take you home again."

Tears of joy came into Tatsinda's brown eyes. "Oh, my prince!" she said. "My prince!"

"Sh-h, here comes the owl again," he warned her.

Skoodoon swooped low. He had a telquit fruit in each of his claws. Begrudgingly and disparagingly, he dropped these at Tatsinda's feet. Then, still flying low, he circled the blue boulder. It was his custom, as soon as darkness came, to light on the ground beside the mighty rock, apply his beak to the

little space between it and the earth, and give his war scream. This was something like being roused by a fire siren in the doorway and never failed to wake the giant promptly.

So before anything could be done to stop him, Skoodoon had circled the boulder and alighted on the ground within the magic circle. Tackatan sprang to his feet, unlimbering his todendart.

But it was too late!

Before the astounded eyes of Tatsinda and the prince, there was a snow flurry of feathers, a burst of music, and the owl was gone!

Yes, he was gone as an owl; as music he continued. He had become a lively tune entirely unfamiliar to Tatsinda and the prince, but you and I would have thought it sounded strangely like "Pop Goes the Weasel" as rendered by a broken bagpipe and a mouth organ. Forever and ever, or at least until something turned him into an owl again, Skoodoon would roam the air: a wandering and jigging tune.

"What has happened?" cried Tatsinda in bewilderment.

"Alas, the owl's used up the magic intended for the giant," said Tackatan. "The last of the magic, too; there's not another speck in all the mountain."

"Alas," agreed Tatsinda. "And our todendarts are powerless against him. What's to be done now?"

"I shall have to ask the wise woman's advice again."

"One moment, though," Tatsinda said. "I've thought of something. The giant and the owl are both nocturnal creatures: they live their lives at night and sleep by day. The owl doesn't (or didn't) like the sun, but the giant, I am certain, fears it mortally. The first thing he did when we came to this place was to dig himself a burrow beside the boulder. And if toward dawn he is a little late returning to it, he looks positively terrified. I think, my prince, if you would conquer the monster, you must subject him to the light of day; he will be clumsy then, at least, and at a disadvantage."

"Excellent advice," said Tackatan admiringly. "I intend to act upon it. But now, Tatsinda, I shall set you free."

"No, wait!" she whispered. "For if the giant wakes and finds the owl and

I have disappeared, who knows what he will do? Go searching in a fury, maybe; crush our villages and harm our people! No, I must stay tethered till a way is found."

"Brave girl!" said Tackatan. There was no time to say more, for suddenly there was the sound of a mighty subterranean yawn; the boulder rocked a bit and was thrust aside. The giant stretched his tree-long arms and stood up; a fearful sight.

He looked about him, glanced absently at Tatsinda, then opened his mouth and bellowed:

"S K O O-D-O-O-O-O-N!"

"...doon,

    oon,

      oon,

        oon," replied the echoes. There was no other answer.

Johrgong shrugged and yawned again, a yawn that rustled all the trees.

"Well," he said in his own tongue. "I suppose the silly chicken has gone to hunt for food again." He said it contemptuously, since he himself cared little for food and had been known to go as long as twenty days without it. "I wonder why he didn't wake me up, though? Oh, well, who cares. Tonight I'll hew the trees to build my sledge."

And soon he was at work, flailing away with his ax. One tree and then another crashed to earth. The timbertocks fled twanging through the forest.

"This is something new," Tatsinda murmured to the prince. "Always before he's worked with pick and shovel, digging up triknix."

"What can he want with all that lumber?" Tackatan wondered. "You don't suppose he's going to build a house and live here all his life, do you?"

"I hope not and I doubt it, since I think his home is underground. But we must wait and see," said Tatsinda philosophically.

For a time they watched and listened to the giant without speaking; Tackatan in his hiding place, Tatsinda tethered to the tree. Then Tackatan said: "I have an idea, Tatsinda. But it will take a while to carry out. First, I must summon together my brothers and our fellow Tatran men. All of them. When day has come, we must somehow, in total silence, push the boulder away and then, Tatsinda, we must snare this giant in a net!"

"How brilliant!" cried Tatsinda, clasping her hands together in admiration.

"But where, oh, where in the mountain shall we find a snare quickly enough that is strong enough and large enough?" said Tackatan, suddenly grave and doubtful.

Tatsinda drew herself up proudly.

"You forget, my prince, that I am a weaver, and a swift one," she said. "If you will bring me strands to work with, you shall have your net before another night is over."

"Remarkable Tatsinda!" exclaimed the prince. "I shall go to Tanda-nan at once and ask what's the best thread for giants. I shall bring it to you and then fetch my cohorts. But," he said hesitatingly, "I do not like to leave you here alone."

"I shall be safe enough. The monster will be hard at work; he is industrious, I will say that for him; and at the first hint of day he will be gone to earth again."

So Tackatan took Tatsinda's hand and kissed it, then reluctantly made his way, under cover of shadows, to the mountain path that led to the wise woman's valley.

Chapter Seven

"You mean to say that the magic was wasted on an *owl?*" exclaimed Tanda-nan in outrage. "An *owl?* Magic that turned the dreaded timbledads to tunes? Magic that saved the mountain from the tendrilled tiskadole, and the cold, creeping, crystal-chewing tixidont? Magic that rendered the bitter tinder-vetter and the gruesome tilg melodious? Oh, that this masterpiece of sorcery should have had its final expression in the alteration of a mere owl!"

"Not mere, Tanda-nan," the prince said gently. "This was the greatest snowy owl that anyone has ever seen, a giant among birds."

"Well, that's a little better," said Tanda-nan, somewhat mollified. "Nevertheless, he's done away with the last of the magic."

"Yes, but we have another plan," Tackatan told her. And he described the project of the snare.

"Timbril silk, that's what you want," Tanda-nan said when he had finished. "Luckily I have a good supply on hand. You never know when you may need it."

The timbril, it should be explained here, was the closest thing to a spider on Tatrajan, and at that its only resemblance to a spider was the fact that it spun silk. It was a pretty, fluffy little creature, but the silk it spun was stronger than a strand of steel and so fine as to be well-nigh invisible; ten thousand yards of it would fill a teacup. And it was ten thousand yards that Tanda-nan now gave the prince.

"Poor girl, it's frightful stuff to work with," she said. "But I shall put my wishes on her and be near at hand, too. I wouldn't miss this spectacle for anything!"

Tackatan thanked the wise woman with all his heart, then hurried away through the shadows to Tatsinda.

During what was left of the night, and all the next day, Tatsinda wove the timbril strands. The slightest breath of air would lift them from her hands, and they had a disposition to cling to things: leaves, twigs, blades of grass. But Tatsinda's skill and patience were both great; and she was swift. The net, so delicate that it was hard to see, grew and grew beneath her flying fingers.

As day wore into afternoon, the Tatrajanni, more than a thousand strong and led by Tackatan, crept up the mountainside and concealed themselves in the forest near the quarry. Johrgong's thunderous snoring masked any rustling they might have made. On the ground beside the boulder, the trees for his sledge, neatly stripped of their boughs, lay side by side. Tonight he would lash them together with tough tempkin vines. Then he would start to load the greb and tomorrow after dark would be on his way. Under the blue boulder he dreamed with pleasure of the chagrin and jealousy he would soon cause Blamrigg, Clangmar, and Gagg.

The day deepened; the shadows gathered. Tired and sleepy, Tatsinda forced herself to stay awake, only allowing herself to stretch her arms now and then before returning to her rapid weaving. Tanda-nan, concealed nearby, watched her with approval.

Now it was dusk. The evening star came out. The hidden Tatrajanni hardly breathed, and the excitement of their waiting seemed to quiver the air . . .

The mammoth snoring had stopped. There was a yawn, a grumble. Then the boulder rocked, was shoved aside, and the giant stood up.

It was hard for the watching Tatrans not to gasp. They had forgotten how immense he was.

Johrgong looked about him. An expression of puzzled displeasure crossed his face. Once again he threw back his shaggy head, opened his shaggy mouth, and roared:

"S K O O · D · O · O · O · O · N!"

". . . doon,

    oon,

       oon,

          oon," replied the echoes as usual. The ambushed Tatrajanni pressed their hands to their ringing ears.

Johrgong's displeased eye fell on Tatsinda. He went over to her and leaned down.

"What has become of the owl?" he demanded before he remembered that she could not understand him. "A plague on you, dolly. Why can't you speak a civilized tongue? If that feathered deserter does not return before sunrise, I'll have to take you into the earth with me. I won't have you running away. Oho, no! Jangborg shall have her dolly yet!"

Tanda-nan listened and watched from her hiding place, and although she could not understand the giant either, she was, we must remember, a wise woman of vast experience, and she had a pretty good idea of what he was saying. She knew what to do about it, too, and, shutting her eyes, she drew into her own mind, imagining with all the concentration of her powers that she was a great white owl. When, for a moment, she was able to believe that she *was* an owl, she opened her mouth and uttered an eerie hunting cry so like that of Skoodoon that even Tatsinda was startled, believing for an instant that the owl, freed from music, had returned.

Johrgong was completely hoodwinked.

"Oh, there you are, Skoo," he called. "I thought for a minute — but never mind."

He was in great good spirits after that and went vigorously about the business of ripping down tempkin vines, bellowing the Greb Song as he

worked. The poor Tatrajanni kept their hands to their ears; all except Tatsinda, who, under cover of darkness, went on with her weaving.

By midnight the snare had been completed, every strand of timbril silk utilized. Then, and only then, Tatsinda lay down on the ground and slept; so tired that Johrgong's uproar could not wake her. From their hiding places the wise woman and the prince watched over her.

All the rest of the night the giant continued to bellow and hum happily. When he had completed the sledge to his satisfaction, he went about the delightful business of loading it and grinned his dreadful grin as he viewed the extent of his treasure.

"Oh, they will be miserable when they see this!" he gloated joyfully. "Oh, they will suffer!"

He was so pleasantly preoccupied that he did not notice the passing of time. A hint of daybreak — not yet light enough to be called light — was altering the dark. It was only when the titchkips, beginning with Tanda-nan's, high on the mountain, and answered by others in the villages and valleys below, began to make their morning sound, their thousand wooden-mallet notes, that he looked up to see the brightening sky. He ran to his burrow, rolled into it, and pulled the boulder over him. Just in time, too: the sun, a fire-rose at that hour, began to show its rising edge.

On the mountain, except for the titchkips and the morning birds, all was still. You would not have guessed that more than a thousand people were hidden in the quiet woods. When King Tagador arrived on his timtik litter, that was quiet, too; the animals' hoofs were hushed with little shoes of tiptod fleece.

The sun rose higher. It was going to be a beautiful day.

Still all was silence. Tatsinda awoke, sat up, and combed her golden hair.

"Good morning," whispered the prince.

"Good morning," whispered Tatsinda.

After a while the giant sounds of Johrgong's sleep began, and not until they had been going on for more than half an hour did the Tatrajanni begin to creep — quietly, quietly! — from their hiding places. Only cats or shadows could have been more quiet.

All had been arranged on the preceding day. It had been decided that the princes, Tamin, Taskin, and Tackatan, would climb up into the branches of the highest, nearest trees. Each would hold an edge of the snare, so that when they were in their places, it would float high above the boulder like a canopy. And then, when at last the boulder was rolled away, they would drop the net over the emerging giant, trapping him. The other Tatrajanni would at once move in, grasping the edges of the snare, shackling him.

But immediately there was trouble. The net of timbril silk, all but invisible against the sky, was so light, so fine, that every air that breathed lifted it high and billowing above the trees. How could anything so airy be dropped to trap a giant?

"Fasten stones to the edges!" commanded Tanda-nan in a low but penetrating voice, waving her staff at Johrgong's greb stones loaded on the sledge. "Use the giant's trash to catch him!"

So the princes climbed down from the trees; and many hastening hands, Tatsinda's among them, worked at tying bright pebbles to the edges of the snare. It took a long time, but finally the task was done, and the princes climbed into their trees again.

The sun was high now. It beamed straight down into the quarry. Fifty of the strongest Tatrajanni converged in silence on the enormous boulder, gathering on its western side. It loomed above them, glinting with blue stabs of light.

There was a waiting, breathless pause. Then at a signal from King Tagador the fifty Tatran men pressed against the stone and pushed with all their strength. Tanda-nan also applied a powerful wish.

Under such mighty impetus the boulder gave way, rolled from its place, gained speed as it rolled, and went slamming like thunder down the mountainside, breaking itself in great blazing fragments as it struck and shattered on other rocks. The noise was stupendous.

The Tatrajanni, swift as swallows, had already leaped backward to safety as Johrgong sat up. First bewildered, then enraged, he opened his mouth in an earsplitting yell of fury. Then he rose to his feet, stepped out of his burrow, and the net dropped over him. The Tatran men sprang forward to seize the edges.

Still dazed from sleep and light, the giant pawed at his transparent snare but could not tear or loosen it. The noonday sun, too bright to look at, looked down at Johrgong steadily. The anger faded from his face; instead he wore an expression of surprise . . . What was happening now?

What was happening was that Johrgong the Gadblang, Johrgong the giant, dreadful and mighty, was beginning to dwindle: slowly at first, then faster and faster and faster until, in five seconds, all that was left of him was a heap of clothes and two big stone shoes. The last that was seen of him was a puff of black smoke—presumably his soul—that rose and vanished in the lighted air.

As they walked slowly down the mountainside, a little apart from the others, Prince Tackatan took Tatsinda's hand in his.

"Tatsinda," he said. "You are the best and bravest girl in all the mountain. Furthermore, you are the most beautiful by far. I have known this for years, and for years I have hoped with all my heart that someday you would be my wife. Could you marry me? Would you marry me, O beautiful Tatsinda?"

Tatsinda wasted not a second in saying that indeed she could and would; and no two people on the mountain or in all the world that lay beyond, for that matter, were happier than they.

"But what of Tamberine?" Tatsinda asked after a moment.

"Oh, Tamberine loves my brother Taskin," replied Tackatan cheerfully. "And he loves her. They are to be married; it's all settled."

After another moment Tatsinda said: "Did you admire the birthday totle I wove for you, my prince?"

And the prince said: "Indeed I have not seen it yet. I had neither time nor heart to open birthday presents. But now all that is changed, and you shall help me open them!"

Tatsinda thought to herself: So I asked Tanda-nan my question without needing to, and I used the magic that she gave me without needing to. The

·62·

answer and the magic were never necessary after all!

And strangely enough, this knowledge made her happier than ever.

On their wedding day, old Tanda-nan came down the mountain for the first time in a hundred and sixty-six years. She came to show her affection and to join in the festivity, wearing a gown of the olden time and a dazzling array of torms: necklaces, bracelets, and ornaments for her ears and anklebones and chin. But no one could outshine Tatsinda in her bridal dress of timbril silk and her crown of nodding tondil flowers. Even the most doubting of the Tatrajanni now saw that she was beautiful.

There was revelry and dancing and music for seven days and seven nights. It was the most glorious celebration that Tatrajan had ever known. And Tatsinda and the prince lived happily ever after.

In time their marriage was blessed with six children: three with snow-white hair and ice-blue eyes, and three with golden hair and velvety brown eyes. In due course these children themselves grew up and married and had children of their own, some of whom had ice-blue eyes and golden hair, and some of whom had *brown* eyes and golden hair; others, of course, had brown eyes and white hair, and still others had *blue* eyes and white hair. And then they grew up and *they* had children, and so on and on and on until this day; and since the Tatrajanni are always beautiful, the only change is that there are many different sorts of beauty in the kingdom now instead of only one.

So for many, many years, more years than I can name or number, the Tatrajanni have lived in peace and usefulness. There is no word in the Tatran language that means boredom. There is no word that means war. There is a word that means hate, but no one uses it except the children, and they use it only in their games.

The rock-crystal villages flash and sparkle in the sun; the timtiks sing as they take the children to school. The people prosper and are happy in their mountain world. No one from beyond the wall of mist has ever come to trouble them again.

And no one ever will.

The illustrations in this book were done in watercolor and ink on
Whatman watercolor paper.
The display type was set in Skjald and Folkwang.
The text type was set in Kennerly Old Style.
Composition by Thompson Type, San Diego, California
Color separations were made by Bright Arts, Ltd., Singapore.
Printed and bound by Tien Wah Press, Singapore
Production supervision by Warren Wallerstein and Ginger Boyer
Designed by Lydia D'moch